ON A MAGICAL DO-NOTHING DAY

For Francesca, who sees the world shine through stones. And for the tiny and the big Mimosa.

Thank you to Tiberio, who inspired this book, and to Veronica, Manu, Pata, John B., Béatrice, Sandro, and Claudia.

BEATRICE ALEMAGNA

On a Magical Do-Nothing Day

Thames & Hudson

Here we were again. Me and Mum
in the same cabin. The same forest.
The same rain. Dad back in the city.

Mum sat at her desk,
quietly writing, while
I destroyed Martians.
Actually, I was just pressing
the same button over and over.

I wished Dad were here.

'What about a break from your game?' Mum growled.
'Is this going to be another day of doing nothing?'

She was right. There was nothing I wanted to do.
Except destroy Martians.

She took the game out of
my hands and hid it, as usual.

I found it, as usual,
and went outside . . .

. . . where it felt like everything in our garden
was hiding from the rain.

I held my game tightly. Maybe it would protect me from this boring, wet place.

I walked down the hill.

At the bottom of our path,
I saw some flat rocks in the pond.

The rocks were round – like the heads of
the Martians. I decided to jump on them
and crush them.

Oh no! What did I do? My game fell in the
pond! This COULD NOT be happening to me!

I stuck my hand into the water to grab it.
It was so icy-cold, I screamed.

Without my game, I had nothing to do.

The rain was so hard it felt like rocks hitting me.

I was a small tree caught in a hurricane.

Just then, there were four lights, and four huge snails appeared.

'Is there anything to do around here?' I asked them.

'Yes, indeed,' they told me.

I reached out and touched their antennae –
they were as soft as jelly.
It made me smile.

I followed them down the path and soon
I found dozens of mushrooms. The air
was so damp. I knew the smell from
when I was small – my grandparents'
basement. My cave of treasures.

I knew that there was something
special close by.
That I was surrounded.

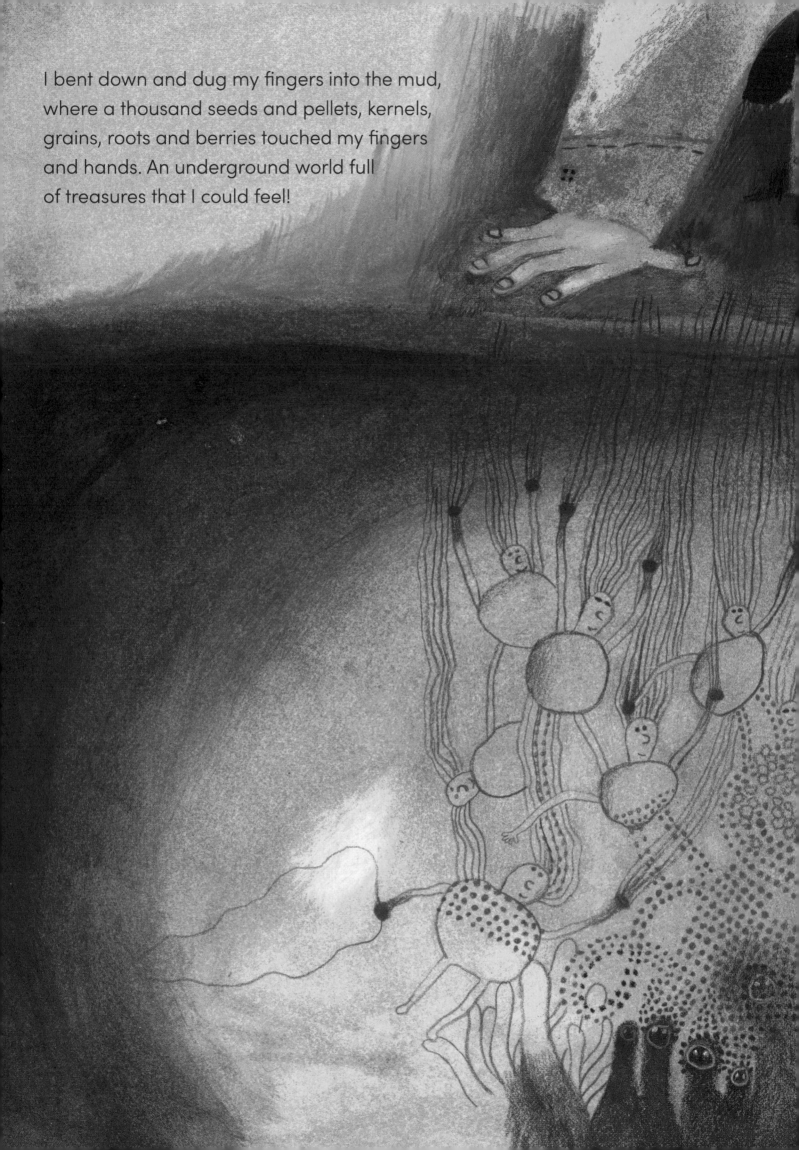

I bent down and dug my fingers into the mud,
where a thousand seeds and pellets, kernels,
grains, roots and berries touched my fingers
and hands. An underground world full
of treasures that I could feel!

I looked up at the sky. Sunbeams fell down through a giant sieve and blinded me.

I thought I heard the beat of drums from far away, but it was just my heart!

I felt filled with energy and began running fast.

So fast, I fell down the hill.

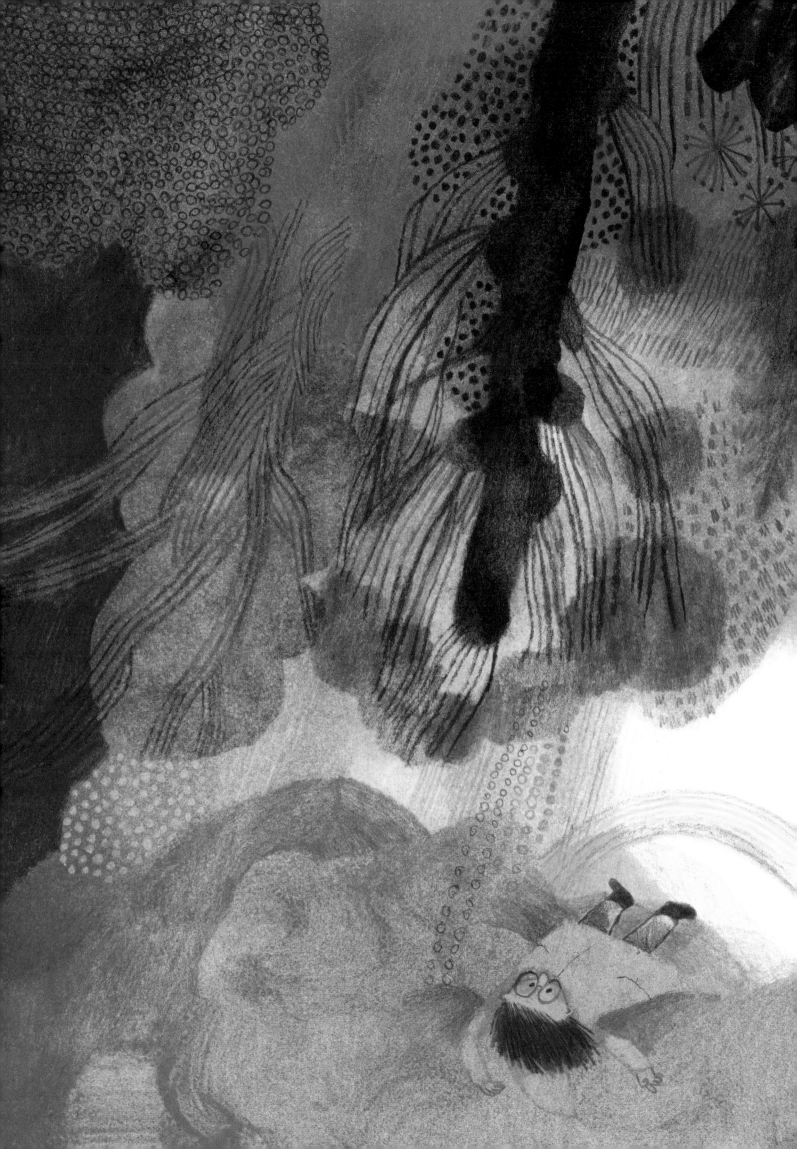

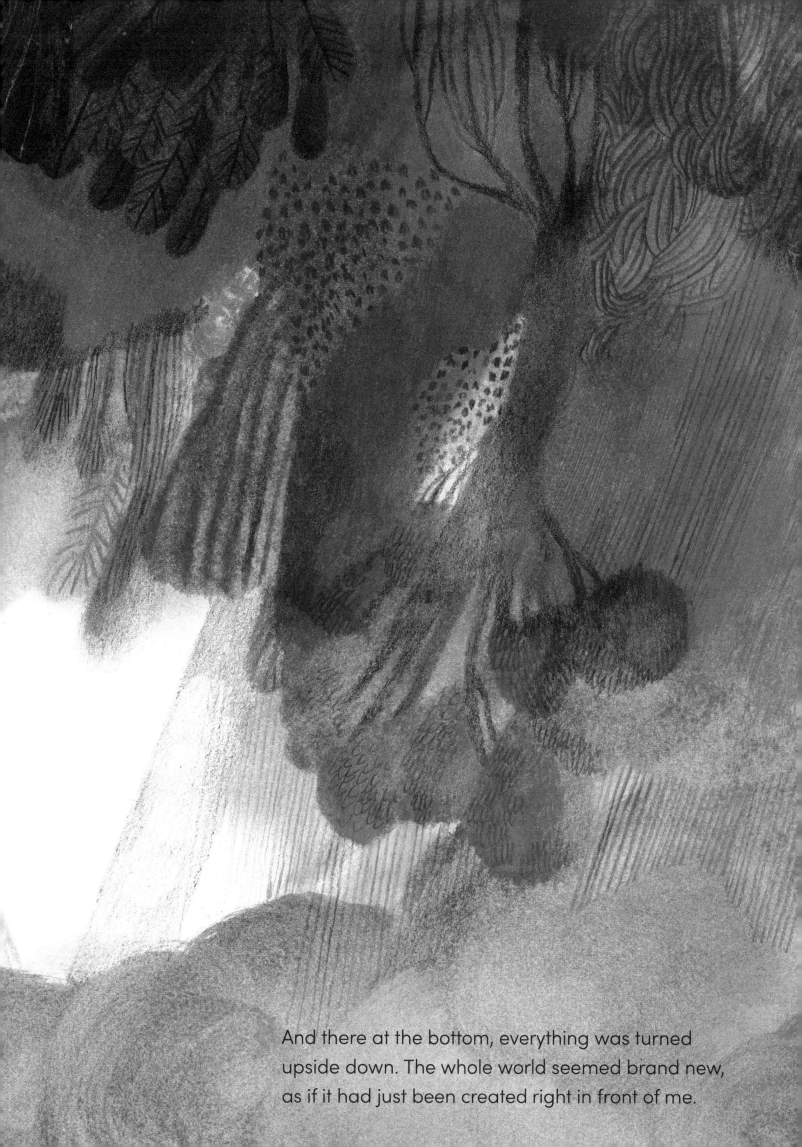

And there at the bottom, everything was turned
upside down. The whole world seemed brand new,
as if it had just been created right in front of me.

I climbed a tree and looked out
as far as my eyes could see.

I breathed in air until my lungs
were bursting.

I drank the raindrops like
an animal would.

I noticed bugs I'd never seen before.

I talked to a bird.

I made my biggest splash,

then I collected smooth stones as clear as glass
and watched the world shining through them.

Why hadn't I done these things before?

Soaked to the bone, I ran inside
the house, took off my coat, and
looked in the mirror.

Ohhh! I thought I saw my dad
smiling at me.

My mother was there, still writing, but now she looked different – like one of the creatures outside.

'Oh! You're soaked through.
Let me dry you.'

She took a towel and we
went to the kitchen.

I felt like giving her a big hug. I wanted to tell her
what I had seen, felt and tasted outside in the world.

But I didn't. We just sat in the kitchen, looked at each other, and breathed in the delicious smell of our hot chocolate.

That's it. That's all we did.

On this magical do-nothing day.

The End

Translated from the French *Un Grand Jour de Rien* by Jill Davis

First published in the United Kingdom in 2017 by
Thames & Hudson Ltd, 181A High Holborn,
London WC1V 7QX

This paperback edition first published in 2018

Published by arrangement with HarperCollins *Children's* Books,
a division of HarperCollins Publishers

British Library Cataloguing-in-Publication Data
A catalogue record for this book is available from
the British Library

ISBN 978-0-500-65179-7

Printed and bound in China

To find out about all our publications, please visit
www.thamesandhudson.com.There you can subscribe
to our e-newsletter, browse or download our current
catalogue, and buy any titles that are in print.